JPIC Scott
Scott, Janine
Cafe cosmos

Treasure Chest Readers

Café Cosmos

Text by Janine Scott
Illustrations by Hannah Wood

Published in 2010 by Windmill Books, LLC
303 Park Avenue South, Suite # 1280, New York, NY 10010-3657

Adaptations to North American Edition © 2010 Windmill Books, Copyright © 2008 by Autumn Publishing

Published in 2008 by Autumn Publishing, A division of Bonnier Media Ltd., Chichester, West Sussex, PO20 7EQ, UK

CREDITS: Text by Janine Scott, Illustrations by Deborah Rigby

Library of Congress Cataloging-in-Publication Data

Scott, Janine.
  Cafe cosmos / text by Janine Scott ; illustrations by Hannah Wood. -- 1st North American ed.
    p. cm. -- (Treasure chest readers)
  Published in Great Britain in 2008 by Autumn Publishing.
  Summary: The cheese-loving owner of the first dairy diner in space invents a new dessert for a finicky customer.
  ISBN 978-1-60754-673-3 (library binding) -- ISBN 978-1-60754-674-0 (pbk.) -- ISBN 978-1-60754-675-7 (6-pack)
  [1. Stories in rhyme. 2. Outer space--Fiction. 3. Cheese--Fiction. 4. Diners (Restaurants)--Fiction. 5. Humorous stories.] I.
Wood, Hannah, ill. II. Title.
  PZ8.3.S4275Caf 2010
  [E]--dc22
                              2009040141

Manufactured in the United States of America

CPSIA Compliance Information: Batch #BW01W: For further information contact Windmill Books, New York, New York at 1-866-478-0556.

alphabet soup™
an imprint of
WINDMILL BOOKS™
New York

The Cosmic Café,
In the wide Milky Way,
Was the first dairy diner in space.

It had comet-shaped chairs,
Bright stars on the stairs
And satellites all around the place.

Mars Mozzarella,
A cheese-loving fellow,
Owned the Cosmic Café.

He grilled cheese for brunch.
He baked cheese for lunch,
And then helped to serve cheese all day.

The café's best waiter
Was a wiz with the grater.
He came from a planet named Brie.

Together they knew
Every cheese dish and stew,
And their cheese sauce was lovely to see.

Then, one afternoon,
The Man in the Moon
Came to the café to eat.

"The moon's made of cheese,
So I don't want that, please.
I'm looking for something quite sweet."

The waiter went red,
Steam shot from his head,
For cheese was his favorite food.

And Mars Mozzarella,
That cheese-loving fellow,
Thought that the Moon Man was rude!

"I'll show him," he thought.
"I'll soon change his mind."
And he rushed to the kitchen to cook.

He started to stir,
To dice, slice, and whir.
And his waiters all stopped by to look.

His sweet cake creation
Soon caused a sensation,
The loveliest thing he had baked.

It was smooth, round, and white,
A cosmic delight,
Like a moon in the shape of a cake.

Soon Mars Mozzarella,
That cheese-loving fellow,
Was famous, a Milky Way star.

They all knew his name,
And everyone came
By spaceship, spacebus, and spacecar.

Now Mars Mozzarella,
That cheese-loving fellow,
Has cafés all over the sky.

His favorite, they say,
Is the Cosmic Café,
But no one has ever guessed why.

Still, each afternoon,
The Man in the Moon
Comes in for his favorite treat.

The café's best waiter
Hides his cheese grater
And brings a moon cake to his seat.

But Mars Mozzarella
Has fooled that Moon fellow.
His special moon cake is a fake.

And one day quite soon,
When there's a blue moon,
He'll tell him that treat is CHEESEcake!

LEARN MORE! READ MORE!

Fun rhymes and rhythm, like the author used in *Café Cosmos*, can help increase your appetite for reading! Here are some more books that use and explore some of those great reading tools.

FICTION
Hicks, Barbara Jean. *Monsters Don't Eat Broccoli*. New York: Knopf Books for Young Readers, 2009.

Thomas, Jan. *Rhyming Dust Bunnies*. New York: Beach Lane Books, 2009.

NONFICTION
Terban, Marvin. *Time to Rhyme: A Rhyming Dictionary*. Honesdale, PA: Boyds Mills Press, 1997

For more great fiction and nonfiction, go to
www.windmillbooks.com.